O9-BTI-970

ROSS MACDONALD

ROARING BROOK PRESS
Brookfield, Connecticut

For Jamie, Daisy, and Lucy

A NEAL PORTER BOOK

Published by Roaring Brook Press
A division of The Millbrook Press, 2 Old New Milford Road, Brookfield, Connecticut 06804

Library of Congress Cataloging-in-Publication Data
MacDonald, Ross.
Another perfect day / by Ross MacDonald. 1st ed.
p. cm.
Summary: What started out as another perfect day for a superhero performing heroic feats suddenly goes awry.
[1. Heroes Fiction.] I. Title.
PZ7.M1513 An 2002
[E] dc21 2002018798

0-7613-1595-0 (trade)
2 4 6 8 10 9 7 5 3 1

0-7613-2659-6 (library binding)
2 4 6 8 10 9 7 5 3 1

Printed in the United States of America
First edition

The morning sun came streaming through Jack's bedroom window.

He got
up and
looked
out . . .

got dressed . . .

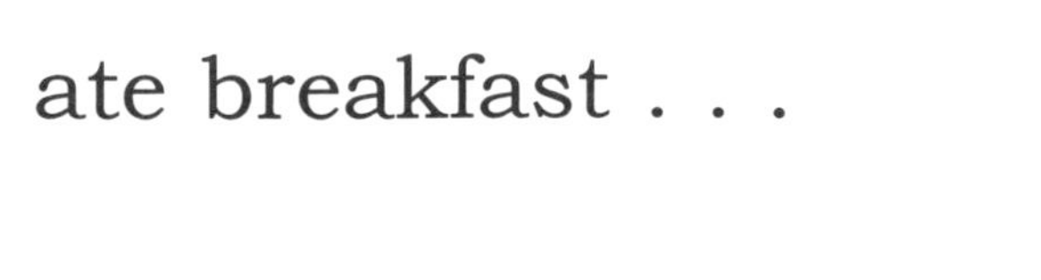

ate breakfast . . .

brushed his teeth . . .

exercised . . .

JACK

and went out.

He stopped
to help out
here . . .

and there . . .

but by now
he was
running
late . . .

so he
caught
the train . . .

to work.

AAAAAAH!
LIFE IS RICH!
CHIEF FLAVOR TESTER
WORLDS BEST ICE CREAM

After work
he decided
to walk home.

But just then . . .

just when he thought
things couldn't
possibly get
any better . . .

they didn't.

In fact, things started to go a little funny.

He went to get his plane . . .
but it looked a little
funny, too!

BEFORE ANYTHING ELSE GOES WRONG...
oh oh...
ZOOM

WHEW! I THINK I LOST THEM!
BUT I DON'T GET IT!
WHY ARE ALL THESE TERRIBLE THINGS HAPPENING?
THIS WAY
WHAT HAPPENED TO MY PERFECT DAY?

YOU DIDN'T WAKE UP YET!
EEEEEEK!

So, Jack tried everything . . .

splashing water on his face . . .

an alarm clock. . . .

EVERYTHING!

IT'S NO USE!
I CAN'T WAKE UP!
PINCH
THAT'S BECAUSE YOU'RE DOING IT ALL WRONG!

FIRST, YOU'VE GOT TO CLOSE YOUR EYES AND THINK ABOUT THE SUNLIGHT STARTING TO COME IN YOUR WINDOW...

AND THE SOUNDS OF BIRDS...
AND THE SMELL OF BREAKFAST BEING MADE...

And sure enough . . .

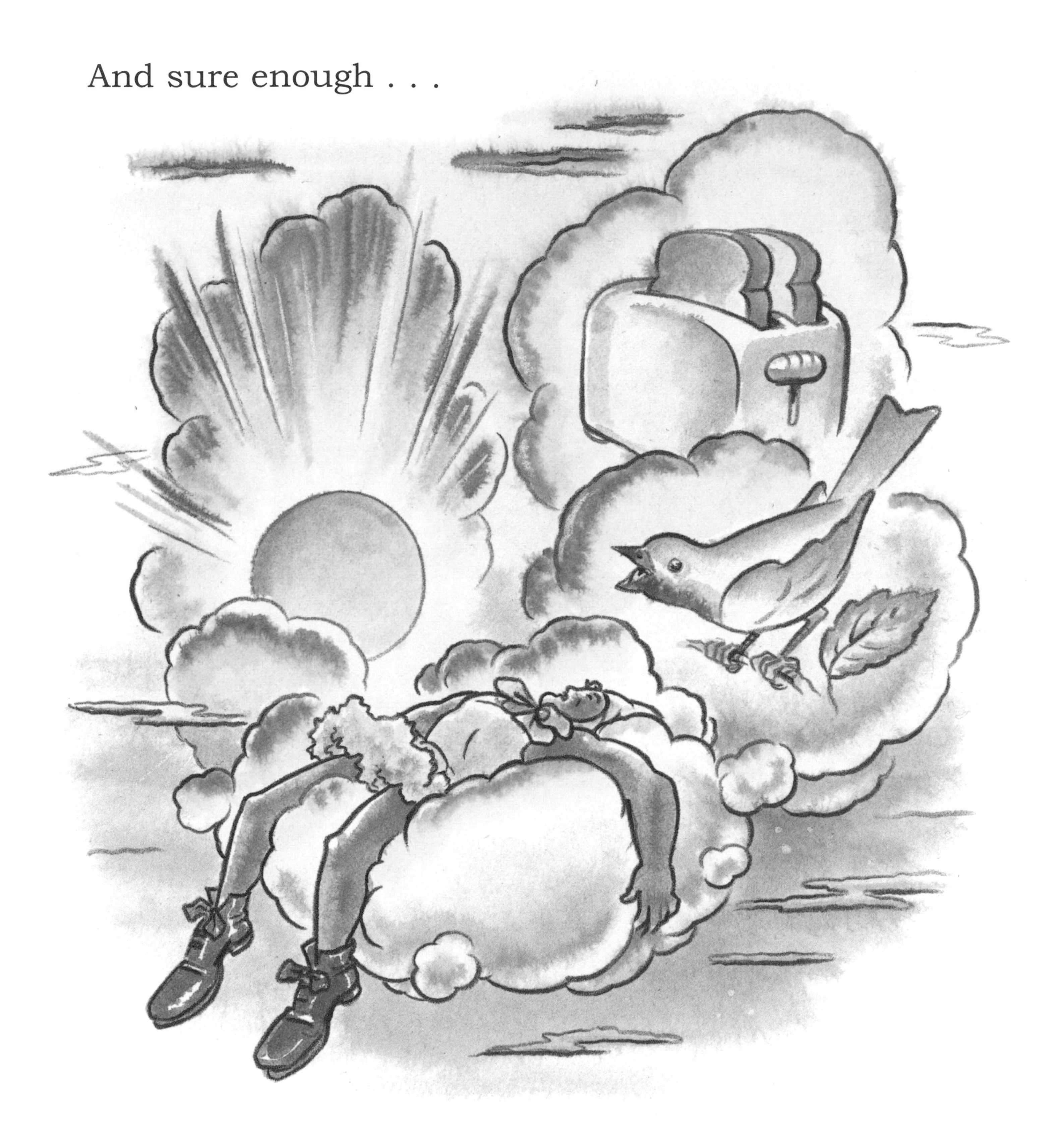

when Jack tried it . . .

he woke up!